Homophobia: From Social Stigma to Hate Crimes

The Gallup's Guide to Modern Gay, Lesbian, & Transgender Lifestyle

Homophobia: From Social Stigma to Hate Crimes

by Bill Palmer

Mason Crest Publishers

MASON CREST PUBLISHERS INC.
370 Reed Road
Broomall, Pennsylvania 19008
(866)MCP-BOOK (toll free)
www.masoncrest.com

First Printing
9 8 7 6 5 4 3 2 1

Library of Congress Cataloging-in-Publication Data
Palmer, Bill, 1957–
Homophobia : from social stigma to hate crimes / by Bill Palmer.
    p. cm.
Includes bibliographical references and index.
ISBN 978-1-4222-1752-8 (hardcover)   ISBN 978-1-4222-1758-0 (series)
ISBN 978-1-4222-1871-6 (pbk.)   ISBN 978-1-4222-1863-1 (pbk series)
1. Homophobia—Juvenile literature. I. Title.
HQ76.4.P35 2011
306.76'6—dc22
                        2010026823

Produced by Harding House Publishing Service, Inc.
www.hardinghousepages.com
Interior design by MK Bassett-Harvey.
Cover design by Torque Advertising + Design.
Printed in the USA by Bang Printing.

PICTURE CREDITS

Contents

Introduction

We are both individuals and community members. Our differences define individuality; our commonalities create a community. Some differences, like the ability to run swiftly or to speak confidently, can make an individual stand out in a way that is viewed as beneficial by a community, while the group may frown upon others. Some of those differences may be difficult to hide (like skin color or physical disability), while others can be hidden (like religious views or sexual orientation). Moreover, what some communities or cultures deem as desirable differences, like thinness, is a negative quality in other contemporary communities. This is certainly the case with sexual orientation and gender identity, as explained in *Homosexuality Around the World*, one of the volumes in this book series.

Often, there is a tension between the individual (individual rights) and the community (common good). This is easily visible in everyday matters like the right to own land versus the common good of building roads. These cases sometimes result in community controversy and often are adjudicated by the courts.

An even more basic right than property ownership, however, is one's gender and sexuality. Does the right of gender expression trump the concerns and fears of a community or a family or a school? *Feeling Wrong in Your Own Body*, as the author of that volume suggests, means confronting, in the most personal way, the tension between individuality and community. And, while a community, family, and school have the right (and obligation) to protect its children, does the notion of property rights extend to controlling young adults' choice as to how they express themselves in terms of gender or sexuality?

Changes in how a community (or a majority of the community) thinks about an individual right or responsibility often precedes changes in the law enacted by legislatures or decided by courts. And for these changes to occur, individuals (sometimes working in small groups) often defied popular opinion, political pressure, or religious beliefs. Some of these trends are discussed in *A New Generation of Homosexuality*. Every generation (including yours!) stands on the accomplishments of our ancestors and in *Gay and Lesbian Role Models* you'll be reading about some of them.

One of the most pernicious aspects of discrimination on the basis of sexual orientation is that "homosexuality" is a stigma that can be hidden (see the volume about *Homophobia*). While some of my generation (I was your age in the early 1960s) think that life is so much easier being "queer" in the age of the Internet, Gay-Straight Alliances, and Ellen, in reality, being different in areas where difference matters is *always* difficult. Coming Out, as described in the volume of the same title, is always challenging—for both those who choose to come out and for the friends and family they trust with what was once a hidden truth. Being healthy means being honest—at least to yourself. Having supportive friends and family is most important, as explained in *Being Gay, Staying Healthy*.

Sometimes we create our own "families"—persons bound together by love and identity but not by name or bloodline. This is quite common in gay communities today as it was several generations ago. Forming families or small communities based on rejection by the larger community can also be a double-edged sword. While these can be positive, they may also turn into prisons of conformity. Does being lesbian, for example, mean everyone has short hair, hates men, and drives (or rides on) a motorcycle? *What Does It Mean to Be Gay, Lesbian, Bisexual, or Transgender?* "smashes" these and other stereotypes.

Another common misconception is that "all gay people are alike"—a classic example of a stereotypical statement. We may be drawn together because of a common prejudice or oppression, but we should not forfeit our individuality for the sake of the safety of a common identity, which is one of the challenges shown in *Gay People of Color: Facing Prejudices, Forging Identities*.

Coming out to who *you* are is just as important as having a group or "family" within which to safely come out. Becoming knowledgeable about these issues (through the books in this series and the other resources to which they will lead), feeling good about yourself, behaving safely, actively listening to others *and* to your inner spirit—all this will allow you to fulfill your promise and potential.

James T. Sears, PhD
Consultant

chapter 1

What's So Scary About Difference?

On the night of October 7, 1998, a University of Wyoming freshman, Matthew Wayne Shepard, met Aaron McKinney and Russell Henderson at the Fireside Lounge in Laramie, Wyoming. The three young men talked and had a few drinks, and at the end of the night, McKinney and Henderson offered Matthew a ride home. It was a ride from hell. Matthew was robbed, beaten, and tortured, then tied to a fence in a remote area overlooking the lights of Laramie. Having found his address in his wallet, McKinney and Henderson planned to burglarize Matthew's apartment. They left him to die, lashed to the fence. Eighteen hours later, Aaron Kriefels found Matthew in a coma and near death. Kriefels at first thought he had come across a beat-up old scarecrow.

Shepard had fractures to his skull and severe brain stem damage. He never regained consciousness and remained on full life support in an intensive care unit at Poudre Valley Hospital in Fort Collins, Colorado. The medical staff at the hospital determined that his injuries were too severe for treatment. He was pronounced dead at 12:53 a.m. on October 12, 1998. He was twenty-one years old.

Matthew Shepard was the son of Dennis and Judy Shepard; he had a younger brother named Logan. Matthew was a bright young man studying political science and was chosen as the student representative for the Wyoming Environmental Council. He had many friends and a close extended family. His father described him as "an optimistic and accept-

The Laramie Project, *a play by Moisés Kaufman and members of the Tectonic Theater Project, was based on hundreds of interviews with people from Laramie, Wyoming about how their lives and their town had been affected by the murder of Matthew Shepard. Here, actors portray members of the Westboro Baptist Church who came to town to picket Matthew's funeral.*

ing young man who had a special gift of relating to almost everyone. He was the type of person who was very approachable and always looked to new challenges." Matthew was also a gay man, well known in his college community for his openness and, as his father said, for his "great passion for equality and . . . for the acceptance of people's differences."

Matthew's murder was quickly identified by the media and members of the Laramie **LGBT** community and their **allies** as a **hate crime**. Aaron McKinney and Russell Henderson were arrested and tried for the crime. At their trial, Chastity Pasley and Kristen Price, girl-friends of McKinney and Henderson, testified that the two men had made a plan to rob a gay man and had gone to the Fireside Lounge that night and selected Matthew Shepard as their victim. But McKinney and Henderson pleaded the "gay panic defense": their lawyers claimed the two men were so terrified by Matthew's **alleged** sexual advances that they were

What's That Mean?

LGBT stands for lesbian, gay, bisexual, and transgender people.

People who support others in a cause are known as *allies*.

A *hate crime* is an illegal act in which the victim is selected because of his or her race, religion, or sexual orientation.

Something that is *alleged* is claimed to be true, but may not be.

driven to temporary insanity, and they were, therefore, not responsible for their actions. Both men were found guilty of felony murder, but Matthew Shepard's father made an emotional statement in the courtroom asking that, in memory of his murdered son's **compassion**, the judge sentence the killers to life imprisonment rather than impose the death penalty.

Tragically, the hate that caused Matthew's death haunted his funeral at St. Mark's Episcopal Church on October 16, 1998. Across the street from the church, members of the Westboro Baptist Church carried signs that read "GOD HATES FAGS" and "MATT SHEPARD ROTS IN HELL."

What's That Mean?

Compassion is the feeling of sympathy and kindness toward another person.

Homophobia is the fear and hatred of homosexuality. A homophobic person is sometimes referred to as a "homophobe."

Homophobia

The death of Matthew Shepard, and the trial of the young men who so brutally murdered him, brought the issue of **homophobia** and its tragic consequences to the attention of the American people as the media closely covered the story. This promising young man, an innocent victim of a hate crime, became a symbol for the many less well-known victims of homophobia in its many forms. But more than ten years later, the number of hate crimes against

Judy Shepard, Matthew Shepard's mother, together with her husband Dennis, founded the Matthew Shepard Foundation to encourage acceptance and equality of LGBT people.

LGBT people continues to rise. According to FBI statistics, there were well over a thousand such crimes reported in 2009—but estimates for the actual number of violent crimes against people identified as gay are much higher, since many states do not legally recognize "gay hate crimes" as a separate category, and many gay people are, for many reasons, afraid to report them. And at the same time that the LGBT community and their allies have been demanding—and slowly gaining—full legal and **civil rights**, their **opponents** on the religious and political **right** have been stepping up their organized efforts against gay rights, using the same homophobic language and arguments that have been used to **oppress** gay people for centuries.

Why, in the twenty-first century, are LGBT people still being denied the rights to housing, to marriage, and to job security that are guaranteed to their fellow citizens? Why are they still in danger

What's That Mean?

The rights of a citizen to personal and political freedom under the law are known as *civil rights*.

Opponents are those who are against something.

In politics and religion, the *right* is the side that is generally against social change and new ideas; a word similar to conservative.

To *oppress* is to keep another person, or a group of people, in an inferior position.

of being harassed, beaten, and even killed on the streets of American cities? Why are they still being condemned from the pulpits of churches and by **conservative** talk show hosts? Why are they still being bullied in the hallways of America's schools, and mocked and **stereotyped** in the media? Progress is being made, but homophobia is still very much alive in our world.

What's That Mean?

Conservative refers to people who like things to stay the same and are resistant to change and new ideas.

When ideas and opinions about people are based on generalizations about the group they belong to, those people are being *stereotyped*.

By playing on people's underlying fears and preaching hatred, anti-gay protesters try to stir the emotions of onlookers.

Some archeologists think that earlier forms of humans might have been hunted and killed off by other groups because they looked and acted differently.

Fear of the Other

It's forty-thousand years ago, on the bitter cold tundra of what is now southwestern France. (Remember—it's the Ice Age!) A group of hungry hunters are tracking a wounded wooly mammoth, an extinct ancestor of the elephant. These hunters are humans, but not quite like us, more thickly built, stronger, and—by our standards—a lot uglier. They are Neanderthals. Meanwhile another group of hunters, this group taller and slenderer and more or less

exactly like us (they are Cro-Magnons) are about to cross paths with the bulky Neanderthals. What's going to happen when they meet? Some archaeologists have theorized that modern humans, like the Cro-Magnons, who had evolved in Africa, killed off the Neanderthals as they moved into their European homeland in an ancient version of *genocide*. They were different, they didn't like the way they looked, and they didn't want to share their hunting grounds with them. The Neanderthals were "the Other," and they became extinct through their contact with modern humans.

There seems to be something deep in the most primitive part of our brain that dislikes, distrusts, and fears "the Other," those people who look or dress or pray or act differently than we do. Time and time again, throughout human history, encounters with "the Other," were, more often than not, hostile and violent. People in one valley hated the people in the next valley for no reason except that they always had. Tribes fought other tribes. Nations fought other nations. Neighboring countries created nasty stereotypes about each other. And religions taught that God was on "our" side and the "other" side was doomed to defeat, and to hell.

Exploration brought the people of the world in contact with each other as never before, but the history of colonization in North and South America

EXTRA INFO

Sociologists have found that people who are prejudiced toward one group of people also tend to be prejudiced toward other groups. In a study done in 1946, people were asked about their attitudes concerning a variety of ethnic groups, including Danireans, Pirraneans, and Wallonians. The study found that people who were prejudiced toward blacks and Jews also distrusted these other three groups. The catch is that Danireans, Pirraneans, and Wallonians didn't exist! This suggests that prejudice's existence may be rooted within the person who feels prejudice rather than in the group that is feared and hated.

During the era of colonization, many Europeans believed that white people were smarter and more important than people of color. In this illustration from the novel Robinson Crusoe, *Crusoe is kind to Friday, the black man, but Friday is clearly in a position of submission to him.*

EXTRA INFO

The Westboro Baptist Church of Topeka, Kansas, and their Pastor Fred Phelps, have been strong opponents of gay rights on the religious right. They held an anti-gay demonstration at Matthew Shepard's funeral. Here's what they say about themselves:

WBC engages in daily peaceful sidewalk demonstrations opposing the homosexual lifestyle of soul-damning, nation-destroying filth. We display large, colorful signs containing Bible words and sentiments, including:

GOD HATES FAGS

FAGS HATE GOD

AIDS CURES FAGS, THANK GOD FOR AIDS

FAGS BURN IN HELL

GOD IS NOT MOCKED

FAGS ARE NATURE FREAKS

GOD GAVE FAGS UP

NO SPECIAL LAWS FOR FAGS

FAGS DOOM NATIONS

THANK GOD FOR DEAD SOLDIERS, FAG TROOPS

GOD BLEW UP THE TROOPS

GOD HATES AMERICA

AMERICA IS DOOMED, THE WORLD IS DOOMED, etc.

Perceiving the modern militant homosexual movement to pose a clear and present danger to the survival of America, exposing our nation to the wrath of God as in 1898 B.C. at Sodom and Gomorrah, WBC has conducted 43,487 such demonstrations since June, 1991, at homosexual parades and other events, including funerals of impenitent sodomites (like Matthew Shepard) and over 200 military funerals of troops whom God has killed in Iraq/Afghanistan in righteous judgment against an evil nation.

(from the Westboro Baptist Church website: www.godthatesfags.com/written/wbcinfo/aboutwbc.html)

and Africa has a tragic theme of racism, slavery, and genocide. While saints and philosophers throughout the ages have tried to help us see the wrongs of turning our fellow human beings into "the Other," dehumanized, feared, and distrusted, our progress as a species toward mutual respect and understanding has been painfully slow.

On a smaller scale, within families and communities, that same primitive part of our brain has long been a factor in how we relate to "the Other." People who are different in any way from the majority have faced **discrimination**, fear, and rejection. Religions have often made the "usual" sacred and the "unusual" evil, while laws and **customs** have rewarded the majority and punished the minority.

What's That Mean?

Discrimination is unfair treatment based on prejudice.

Customs are ideas and ways of doing things that are valued by a society.

Prejudice

The root word of prejudice is "pre-judge." Prejudiced people judge others based purely on the fact that they are "Other," because they belong to a different group than themselves; they make assumptions about others that may have no basis in reality.

They believe that if a person's skin is a different shade—or if a person speaks a different language or wears different clothes or worships God in a different way—or falls in love in a different way—then they already know that person is not as smart, not as nice, not as honest, not as valuable, or not as moral as they are. In fact, they're pretty sure that person is stupid, inferior, dishonest, and downright BAD.

Why do human beings have these feelings? *Sociologists* believe humans have a basic tendency to fear anything that's unfamiliar or unknown. Ever since the Cro-Magnons ran into the Neanderthals, we humans have been assuming that if someone is strange (in that they're not like us), then that person is also scary; they're automatically a threat to us.

If we get to know the strangers, of course, we end up discovering that they're not so different from ourselves; they're not so frightening and threatening

People sometimes use graffiti as an anonymous way to give their opinion.

after all. But too often, we don't let that happen. We put up a wall between the strangers and ourselves. We're on the inside; they're on the outside. And then we peer over the wall, too far away from the people on the other side to see anything but our differences.

The idea of "the Other" continues to support racism, **sexism,** homophobia and prejudice of all kinds. It holds us back from the progress we need to make as human beings on this planet. Stereotypes, misunderstandings, and ignorance have kept us from being able to appreciate that it is in honoring our **diversity** and our unique individual qualities that we strengthen our communities and support the health and safety of our Earth. We need to try to get beyond that primitive part of our brain that fears and rejects diversity and get to know each other better. That's the only way to get past prejudice.

What's That Mean?

Prejudice based on a person's being either male or female is called **sexism**.

Diversity refers to people in all their variety of race, behavior, and characteristics.

FIND OUT MORE ON THE INTERNET

The Concept of "the Other"
academic.brooklyn.cuny.edu/english/melani/cs6/other.html

Homophobia in Schools
www.365gay.com/news/homophobia-in-schools-remains-major-problem

The Matthew Shepard Foundation Website
www.matthewshepard.org/site/PageServer

READ MORE ABOUT IT

Fishbein, Harold D. *Peer Prejudice and Discrimination: The Origins of Prejudice.* Mahwah, N.J.: Lawrence Erlbaum, 2002.

Patterson, Romaine, and Patrick Hinds. *The Whole World Was Watching: Living in the Light of Matthew Shepard.* Los Angeles: Alyson Books, 2005.

chapter 2

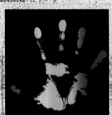

Homophobia and Its Victims

Homophobia is a particular kind of prejudice. It's the fear of the Other when that other person's sexual behaviors are different from your own. The suffix "phobia" refers to feelings of intense fear and hatred—so "homo" + "phobia" means fear and hatred of homosexuals.

How Common Is Homosexuality?

Estimates vary as to the number of gay and lesbian people in the population, but many studies estimate that as many as 10 percent of American adults identify themselves as gay. That's one in ten people! To put it another way, about the same number of Americans are gay as are left-handed. (If you're gay *and* left-handed, you're a double minority.) What that means is that there are literally millions of our fellow citizens who are being stereotyped, discriminated against, denied their full civil rights, and even facing the threat of violent hate crimes simply because of their **sexual orientation**, simply because they are gay or lesbian. Homophobia is negatively affecting the lives of millions of people; people in your community, people you know, people you care about, maybe even you. Gay people are everywhere and, unfortunately, so is homophobia.

Scientists have discovered that same-sex sexual behavior is very common in the animal kingdom, of which human beings are a part. Homosexuality has been observed in close to 1,500 species and is well-documented in over five hundred, including black swans, mallard ducks, and penguins, all the apes, elephants, giraffes, sheep, hyenas, lizards, and even fruit flies! Same-sex penguin pairs mate for life and sometimes even raise orphaned chicks together. Researcher Petter Bøckman has written, "No species has been found in which homosexual behavior has not been shown to exist, with the exception of species that never have sex at all, such as sea urchins." While some homophobic people say that homosexuality is a "crime against nature," nature seems to feel differently!

Ancient art (for example, the beautiful images of affectionate couples painted on Greek pottery thousands of years ago) and literature provide clear evidence that same-sex attraction and love has been around for a long, long time. And anthropologists,

What's That Mean?

A person's physical and emotional attraction to either males or females (or both) is their *sexual orientation*.

This group in San Francisco marches to call for the legalization of gay marriage in California.

who study human societies around the world, have found same-sex behavior in just about all of them.

The History of Homophobia

Prejudice against gay people has not existed in all times and places. Far from it. Among certain Native American tribes, "two-spirit people" (people who embodied both sexes) were highly respected as priests and healers. The early Christian Church, as uncovered by the research of Yale University historian John Boswell, had official rites for the blessing of gay marriages. And in much of modern Western Europe, gay people have achieved full legal rights and full acceptance as respected members of their communities.

But homophobia runs deep in **Western culture** and in the Judeo-Christian and Islamic religious traditions. In the ancient legal code of the Jewish people, preserved in the Book of Leviticus in the Jewish and Christian Bible, a man "lying" with another man was punishable by death. And in the twenty-first century, some Jews and Christians still use these three-thousand year old tribal laws of the Hebrew people—with the claim that they were dictated by God— to support their homophobia,

What's That Mean?

Western culture is the civilization of Europe and the countries (the United States, Australia, Canada, etc.) most influenced by Europe.

without any concern about ignoring the same legal code's equally strict rules in many other areas of human behavior. Homophobes can be very selective in the authorities they quote, even when it's God!

While ancient Rome was generally accepting of homosexuality, things changed under the influence of Christianity. The Emperor Constantius declared same-sex marriage illegal in the year 342, and the Christian emperors Valentian II, Theodosius I, and Arcadius declared homosexual sex to be illegal and those who were guilty of it were condemned to be publicly burned alive. The emperor Justinian (526–575) claimed that homosexuals were responsible for famines and earthquakes, just as the Romans had blamed Christians for all kinds of troubles in earlier centuries.

What's That Mean?

An *interpretation* is a particular understanding of something.

For the next thousand and more years, laws based on a particular *interpretation* of the Bible (and as we saw in the previous chapter, a general "primitive brain" fear and distrust of people who are different from the majority) encouraged homophobia and hate crimes. While only enforced at certain times and in certain places, these laws brought people accused of homosexuality before the courts, with punishments

This knight and his servant are being burned at the stake in medieval Switzerland for having a homosexual relationship.

ranging from jail sentences to public whippings to burning at the stake. Homosexuals were punished as criminals and sinners in old Europe in exactly the same way, and with the same Biblical authority, as were Jews and *heretics*. Meanwhile, great artists such as Leonardo Da Vinci and Michelangelo, men who were making enormous contributions to art and culture during this era, may possibly have been homosexuals.

The early settlers of America brought their traditions and their prejudices with them. Strict laws against same-sex behavior, including the death penalty, were enacted in the Colonies. **Sodomy** laws, applying equally to gay and to straight people but usually used only against gays, still remained on the books in many U.S. states in the twenty-first century!

With an increase in the understanding of scientific principles in the 1900s, what had been considered "sinful" behavior in the past (like being gay) began to be seen as a normal part of human behavior. Early sex researchers like Magnus Hirschfield (1868–1935) in Germany argued that since homosexual behavior was just another human activity and did not hurt other people, it was simply not logical—and was in fact, morally wrong—to punish it as a crime. Whether or not it was a "sin" was the problem of religious groups, Hirschfield believed, and should be completely separate from the concerns of government and law.

The *liberal* principles supported by the new science of psychology and the call for increasing human rights for minorities was making some progress, especially in Europe—and then the Nazis came to power in Germany in the 1930s. Like Jews, gypsies, Communists, and other minorities, gay people were *persecuted* as "unfit to live" in Nazi-occupied Europe. Arrested and sent to concentration camps, thousands of gay people were executed or died from disease and starvation in the camps. They were forced to wear the pink triangle on their prison uniform, which often set them apart for particularly brutal treatment.

And while American soldiers—quite a few of them gay and lesbian—had fought bravely in World

What's That Mean?

Liberal refers to new ideas that support social change.

A *persecuted* group of people is mistreated and oppressed.

What's That Mean?

Liberation is the act of being set free from oppression and persecution.

War II (1939–1945) for the principles of human **liberation**, they returned home to a country that was still racist, sexist, and homophobic. In the 1950s and '60s, men and women who gathered together in bars and clubs were subject

Almost all of these signs for a gay pride rally in Paris were vandalized in this way. The sign reads, "This changes nothing for you, and it's important for us."

to police raids, arrest, and public exposure. People's personal lives and careers were destroyed simply for being caught dancing with a member of their own sex. Hate crimes against gay people—robbery, violence, and harassment—went unreported because of

EXTRA INFO

From the United States Holocaust Museum: Persecution of Homosexuals by the Nazis 1933–1945:

- Under Paragraph 175 of the criminal code, male homosexuality was illegal in Germany. The Nazis arrested an estimated 100,000 homosexual men, 50,000 of whom were imprisoned.
- During the Nazi regime, the police had the power to jail indefinitely—without trial—anyone they chose, including those deemed dangerous to Germany's moral fiber.
- Between 5,000 and 15,000 gay men were interned in concentration camps in Nazi Germany. These prisoners were marked by pink triangle badges and, according to many survivor accounts, were among the most abused groups in the camps.
- Nazis interested in finding a "cure" for homosexuality conducted medical experiments on some gay concentration camp inmates. These experiments caused illness, mutilation, and even death, and yielded no scientific knowledge.

After someone vandalized this car, the owner repainted it. Rather than simply paint over the graffiti, she used the word that had been scrawled across her car in a design to show that she is proud of who she is and refuses to hide her lifestyle in fear.

gay people's fear of public exposure and law enforcement's own homophobia. Religious leaders preached against homosexual "sinners," families disowned and rejected their own gay sons and daughters, and gay people were oppressed and humiliated by laws that excluded and denied them their basic rights and protections as citizens. Most gay people led lives of secrecy and denial in order to escape punishing social **stigma** and legal prosecution. The religious, legal, and medical **establishments** were united in their homophobia. In fact, homophobia was completely **institutionalized** in America. And it would take a strong and brave gay liberation movement, starting in the 1970s, to begin the long battle against institutionalized homophobia.

What's That Mean?

A mark of shame is called a *stigma*.

The *establishment* is the people who hold influence and power in society.

Ideas and ways of doing things that are accepted without question by the majority of people are *institutionalized*.

FIND OUT MORE ON THE INTERNET

Homophobia, Prejudice & Attitudes to Gay Men and Lesbians
www.avert.org/homophobia.htm

Nazi Persecution of Homosexuality
www.ushmm.org/museum/exhibit/online/hsx

The Two Spirit Tradition in Native American Experience
www.gay-art-history.org/gay-history/gay-customs/native-american-homosexuality/two-spirit-native-american-gay.html

READ MORE ABOUT IT

Aldrich, Robert. *Gay Life & Culture: A World History*. New York: Rizzoli, 2006.

Rogers, Jack. *Jesus, the Bible, and Homosexuality*. Louisville, Ky.: Westminster John Knox Press, 2009.

chapter 3

An Ongoing Struggle for Rights and Respect

The struggle against homophobia is part of a larger movement toward human liberation that has been a major, positive theme in recent history. It has been a battle by *minority groups* for recognition by the majority, a call for equality under the law, and a reaction against the "primitive brain's" fear and hatred of "the Other" that has caused so much conflict and unhappiness in the history of the world. The battle has been fought in communities, in law courts and legislatures around the world, and—just as important—in the hearts and minds of people. It is a continuing struggle of which we are all a part.

An Era of Change

The decade of the 1960s was a time of great social change in America and around the

What's That Mean?

Minority groups are smaller groups of people within the larger, majority population who differ from the majority in race, religion, sexual orientation, or other characteristics

world. The Civil Rights movement, under the brilliant leadership of Dr. Martin Luther King, Jr., fought for the rights of African Americans who had suffered inequality, oppression, and **segregation** for over two centuries. By organizing, demonstrating, and standing up for themselves, African Americans made sure that their government and their fellow citizens took their demands for full civil rights seriously. And they made tremendous political and social progress while teaching the world, in the phrase of the time, that "Black is Beautiful!"

This LGBT activist uses an echo of Martin Luther King Jr.'s "I Have a Dream" speech to call for gay rights and acceptance.

Young people across America were opening their minds to new ideas. Hippies danced in the parks and called for peace and "flower power," college students protested an unpopular war in Vietnam, while in Vietnam many servicemen seriously questioned what business their government had sending them there. It was an exciting time in America; an era of **idealism**, experimentation, and social change. Freedom was in the air. And the influence of both the African-American Civil Rights movement and the freedom-loving youth culture of the 1960s encouraged minority groups of all kinds to begin to freely express themselves in new ways. Movements for human liberation questioned the old **assumptions** of the establishment and called for a new society where difference and diversity would be celebrated, not feared. If black was beautiful, weren't brown and red and yellow beautiful, too? Didn't women deserve the same rights as men? Gay people, many of whom had been involved in the Civil Rights and youth culture movement, began to ask each other: "What about us?"

What's That Mean?

Idealism is the belief that new ideas can bring about positive changes in people's lives and in society.

Assumptions are beliefs that are based on certain set ideas that may or may not be true.

Forty years after the Stonewall Riots, the Stonewall Inn is still open for business. The sign reads, "Where Pride Began."

At 1:20 a.m. on June 28, 1969, police raided the Stonewall Inn in Greenwich Village, New York City. In 1969, it was illegal for people of the same sex to dance with each other in a public place, to hold hands, or to wear clothes that were not considered "normal" for their sex. Undercover police would come into gay bars and clubs and close them down. If the customers weren't lucky enough to slip out the back door, they were subject to arrest for "disorderly conduct" or "lewd behavior" and their names listed in the newspaper. The average New York gay bar was being raided once a month in the late 1960s, and the authorities were constantly bullying gay people.

But this night was different. Gathering on the street in front of the Stonewall, a group of angry people— including a number of transgender "drag queens" who had been the particular victims of the police— refused to be bullied. Fights broke out between the police and the crowd, windows were broken, parking meters smashed, and many arrests were made in what became known as "the Stonewall Riots."

Many historians consider the Stonewall Riots the beginning of the modern gay rights movement. Within days of the riots, a new political action group was formed in New York. Unlike the more secretive names of earlier homosexual rights groups—like the Mattachine Society and Daughters of Bilitis—this one came right out and proudly called itself the Gay Liberation Front.

The gay liberation movement, with its beginnings in the human liberation movements of the 1960s and

1970s, had three major goals: to encourage gay and lesbian people to be proud of who they are, to organize politically to demand full civil rights and equality under the law, and to educate the general public about gay people. The battle against homophobia was, and still is, a movement that is both political—working hard to make changes in the legal and governmental establishment—and social. The political realm and the social world go hand-in-hand in all human liberation movements. Laws and institutions need to be changed at the same time that the hearts and minds of people need to be won over to understanding, *tolerance*, and respect for diversity.

The 1970s was an exciting time for gay and lesbian people. Gay Pride was an important part of growing gay communities in cities and towns across America. Gay people were encouraged to deal with the hurt of their own *internalized* homophobia and to express their "gayness" proudly and openly

Men in New York City march for gay rights at the 1976 Democratic National Convention.

by identifying themselves to the world as gay men and women. This process was called "coming out of the closet"—in other words, these men and women would no longer hide their true identities out of sight. It was a brave and risky thing to do, especially in the early days of gay liberation.

Laws and institutions had not caught up with the social movement of "out-and-proud" gay people, however. Coming out could mean rejection from family and friends, the loss of a person's job, and an even greater chance of being a victim of homophobia and hate crimes.

An Ongoing Struggle for Rights and Respect   45

But these openly gay **pioneers** made a tremendous difference in helping to change how the rest of the world saw gay people. Instead of people living in the shadows, a scary, disliked "Other," all of a sudden gay people were coming out everywhere—in all their diversity—and really, once you could get a look at them, it turned out they were not so very different from everybody else! If every gay person came out, some people say, there would be no longer be any such thing as homophobia. Doctors, teachers, athletes, politicians, movie stars, aunts, uncles, parents, friends, people we love and admire: gay people are an important part of just about everyone's life.

What's That Mean?

Pioneers are people who are the first to try new things and experiment with new ways of life.

Something that gives strength and energy is said to be **empowering**.

The AIDS Crisis

The AIDS crisis of the 1980s and '90s was both devastating and **empowering** to the gay community. First identified as a "gay men's disease," early AIDS patients received poor medical care. A tremendous social stigma was attached to the disease as gay men became identified with a terrifying, deadly disease. "GAY" now equaled "AIDS" in the minds of many people. Some religious hate groups spread the idea that the disease was a judgment, and a punishment by an angry God against the homo-sexual lifestyle. Hate crimes increased on the streets of cities across America. Sick gay men were evicted from their apartments, rejected by their families, and refused medical treatment. Funding for AIDS research was delayed for years because the disease was seen as affecting groups of people that the majority didn't care much about, gay people, IV-drug users, and the poor.

What's That Mean?

Someone who is *radical* has extreme, out-of-the-ordinary ideas and beliefs.

But the gay community organized to care for its own people and went into action. "AIDS buddies" cooked meals, walked dogs, and took AIDS patients to their medical appointments. The Gay Men's Health Crisis (GMHC) was founded by a group of gay doctors and community leaders in New York City in January of 1982; it was the world's first—and became the leading—provider of HIV/AIDS education, prevention, and care. Frustrated and angered by the lack of government action in educating the general public about HIV/AIDS and in funding research and social programs, the AIDS Coalition to Unleash Power (ACT UP) was organized in 1987. The members of ACT UP were gay and proud and *radical* in their activities; they demanded that they be heard, they demanded that people with HIV/AIDS and their needs be taken seriously, they demanded that LGBT people have the

EXTRA INFO

Congress passed the Matthew Shepard Hate Crimes Prevention Act on October 22, 2009, and President Barack Obama signed it into law on October 28, 2009. Named in honor of the young man who was brutally murdered in a hate crime in Wyoming in 1998, the act expands the 1969 United States federal hate-crime law (which protected victims of hate crimes based on race or religion) to include crimes motivated by a victim's actual or perceived gender, sexual orientation, gender identity, or disability. The act gives federal authorities, like the FBI, greater authority to investigate hate crimes motivated by homophobia, and it provides funding for state and local law enforcement to pursue and prosecute those who commit these crimes. The act is the first federal law to extend legal protections to LGBT victims of hate crimes, and it was supported by thirty-one state Attorneys General and over 210 national law enforcement, professional, education, civil rights, religious, and civic organizations. A November 2001 poll by the Human rights Campaign indicated that 73 percent of Americans were in favor of hate-crime legislation covering sexual orientation.

same rights as any other citizen of the United States. They were committed to political action directed toward politicians and government agencies and to high-impact educational programs. More than twenty years later, they are still at it!

Since his presidency began in 2009, Barack Obama has been expanding the rights of LGBT people, signing the Matthew Shepard Hate Crime Act and extending greater hospital visitation rights to same-sex partners, among other things. Some members of the LGBT community, however, are frustrated that larger steps are not being taken more quickly.

The gay community entered the twenty-first century strong and proud. Gays and lesbians were being portrayed in movies and on television in more realistic ways as more and more gay people came out and demanded to be recognized as who they really are. Some of the most powerful homophobic institutions, like medicine and the church, committed themselves to reform their outdated prejudices. (As early as 1972, the American Psychiatric Association declared that homosexuality was a normal human behavior and that gay people were not "sick," and various religious denominations—Reformed Jews and Episcopalians for example—have been working hard to fully welcome and empower gay people in their congregations.)

What's That Mean?

Something that is accepted, understood, and supported by the majority of people is said to be *mainstream*.

In a "two steps forward and one step back" kind of way, gay people and their allies have seen victories in the courts at the state and federal level, expanding and protecting their rights as citizens. In many ways, gay people have become **mainstream** in modern society.

But while acceptance of gay people and support for their rights continues to grow, the backlash from homophobic political and religious groups still gets

As of 2010, the AIDS Memorial Quilt was considered the largest piece of community folk art in the world. Each panel of the quilt has been created and submitted in memory of one or more people who have died of AIDS or AIDS-related causes. This photo shows one thousand panels of the quilt, displayed in Washington, D.C. in 2004. As of 2010, the quilt had over 46,000 panels and included over 91,000 names.

At a Gay Pride Parade in San Francisco in January 2010, LGBT advocates face off against anti-gay protesters. The anti-gay protesters, from the Westboro Baptist Church, hold signs saying "God Hates You" and "America Is Doomed." The people facing them hold signs saying "God Is Love" and "We 4Give You."

in the way of progress and continues to influence public opinion. Gay people are still the victims of violence and prejudice, and they still have a long way to go before they reach full equality politically and full acceptance in the hearts and minds of the majority.

FIND OUT MORE ON THE INTERNET

LGBT Rights by Country or Territory
en.wikipedia.org/wiki/LGBT_rights_by_country_or_territory

Those Who Lived the Struggle to End Segregation Now Speak Out for Same-Gender Marriage Equality
www.soulforce.org/article/766

What Is Homophobia?
www.adl.org/hate-patrol/homophobia.asp

READ MORE ABOUT IT

Carter, David. *Stonewall: The Riots that Sparked the Gay Revolution.* New York: St. Martin's Press, 2004.

Stevens, Tracy. *How to Be a Happy Lesbian: A Coming Out Guide.* Asheville, N.C.: Amazing Dreams, 2006.

chapter 4

What Can YOU Do About Homophobia?

Young people, both gay and straight, are growing up in a world where the full social acceptance of LGBT people is advancing with an energy never seen before in history. Opinion polls indicate that young people support such gay rights issues as same-sex marriage and adoption rights in numbers far greater than their parents' and grandparents' generations. And positive gay models are everywhere: in the sports and entertainment industry, in politics and religion, in your neighborhood, in your classroom, and in your family. Teenagers are coming out as gays or lesbians in large numbers, supported by Gay-Straight Alliances and anti-homophobia education programs in many schools. In many ways, this may be the best time ever to be an LGBT kid!

And yet we know that middle schools and high schools are not easy places to be different. Peer pressure dominates the social world of adolescents.

These Polish students are participating in the International Day of Silence, protesting how LGBT people have been harassed, abused, and silenced in schools.

Teenagers have always split themselves into groups: the popular kids, the jocks, the science nerds, the partiers. A strong loyalty to your particular group is a big part of being a teenager. One group can decide it dislikes another group. Gossip can hurt people. And nothing hurts a young person more than rejection by their peers. Where do gay and lesbian kids (or kids who think they might be gay) fit into your school and social worlds?

The International Day Against Homophobia and Transphobia is held every year on May 17, around the world. The event provides an opportunity to celebrate diversity of all kinds and encourage respect for all people.

Studies show that LGBT kids still have it rough. One study of 192 gay teenage boys found that one-third of them reported being verbally abused by one or more family members when they came out, and another 10 percent reported being physically assaulted. In a nationwide study of over 9,000 gay high school students, 24 percent of the boys reported being *victimized*, verbally or physically at least *ten times* in the previous school year because of their sexual orientation; 11 percent of lesbians reported the same thing. Gay teenagers are four times more likely to be threatened with a deadly weapon than their straight peers. Teenage victims of homophobia often experience severe depression, a sense of helplessness, low self-esteem, and even suicidal thoughts (LGBT teenagers are almost five times more likely to attempt suicide than straight teenagers). And the negative family, school, and social pressures gay teenagers face can lead them to abuse drugs and alcohol, engage in unsafe sexual activity, and have body image and eating disorders. Not a pretty picture, is it?

If you're a straight teenager, are you contributing to the unhappiness and insecurity, physically and

What's That Mean?

To be **victimized** is to experience unfair and negative treatment, like violence or bullying.

emotionally, of gay and lesbian kids in your school and community? Are YOU homophobic? Ask yourself:

- Do I have negative stereotypes of gay people?
- Do I participate in bullying or making fun of gay kids in my school, or allow it to happen even if I think it's wrong?
- Do I use hurtful language (like "fag" or "dyke") when talking about gay people? Or use the word "gay" in a negative way to mean something uncool?
- Do I tell **offensive** jokes about gay and lesbian people? Or laugh at them?
- Do I *not* treat gay and lesbian people with the same politeness and respect that I expect from other people?

What's That Mean?

Something that is *offensive* hurts other people's feelings, embarrasses them, or encourages negative stereotypes.

If you answered "yes" to any of these questions, you may have to admit to yourself that you are homophobic, and that your dislike or fear of LGBT people is a part of an unfair system that oppresses and excludes people just because of who they are, and who they happen to want to love.

Think about whether or not you really want to be a part of that tired old system of racism, sexism, and

*This student is protesting Proposition 8, the California Marriage
Protection Act, which denied same-sex couples the right to marry. In a
larger way, though, the student is also protesting hatred in general.*

EXTRA INFO

What's with kids using the word "gay" as an insult?

The use of "gay" as a negative adjective is an increasingly common practice in American culture. Many children and adults use the term to refer to anything bad, weak, or otherwise undesirable. Although kids may not have bad intentions when they say it, such language only reinforces the idea that "gay" = "bad." Also, the language can do significant damage to gay and lesbian students, who are forced to endure such language with little recourse.

(Adapted from Nickelodeon ParentsConnects.com)

homophobia that has victimized innocent people and kept human beings apart for so long. It's the twenty-first century, and you are a global citizen of the future. Be proud of who you are—and let people who are different from you be proud, too. Support understanding and freedom and love, they are the things that make life worth living. Do your part to help build a happy and healthy future for the people of the Earth—for all of us. Think about what side you want to be on!

If you're a gay or lesbian teenager, take care of yourself physically and emotionally. Build yourself a support network. Concentrate on the people who love and appreciate you, and try not to worry about the people who don't understand how unique and wonderful you really are. There is no reason for you to feel alone or "abnormal" in a world where millions of gay people are living happy and proud lives, finding love, and doing good work in their communities. Gay people have come a long way, thanks to the bravery and sacrifices of those who have gone before them. Be proud, be happy, and—together with your straight allies—fight homophobia!

FIND OUT MORE ON THE INTERNET

The Gay-Straight Alliance Network
gsanetwork.org/

High School Students Explore Effects of Homophobia
blog.mattalgren.com/2009/01/high-school-students-explore-effects-homophobia/

READ MORE ABOUT IT

Huegel, Kelly. *GLBTQ: The Survival Guide for Queer and Questioning Teens.* Minneapolis, Minn.: Free Spirit Publishing, 2003.

Pascoe, D. J. *Dude, You're a Fag: Masculinity and Sexuality in High School.* Berkeley: University of California Press: 2003.

BIBLIOGRAPHY

Aldrich, Robert. *Gay Life & Culture: A World History.* New York: Rizzoli, 2006.

The American Gay Rights Movement: A Timeline. www.info-please.com/ipa/A0761909.html (16 June 2010).

Carter, David. *Stonewall: The Riots that Sparked the Gay Revolution.* New York: St. Martin's Press, 2004.

Fishbein, Harold D. *Peer Prejudice and Discrimination: The Origins of Prejudice.* Mahwah, N.J.: Lawrence Erlbaum, 2002.

Gay-Straight Alliance Network, gsanetwork.org/ (15 June 2010).

History of the Gay Rights Movement in the US, www.lifeintheusa.com/people/gaypeople.htm (15 June 2010).

Huegel, Kelly. *GLBTQ: The Survival Guide for Queer and Questioning Teens.* Minneapolis, Minn.: Free Spirit Publishing, 2003.

Johnson, Ramon. "How Many Gay People Are There? Gay Population Statistics." About.com Guide, gaylife.about.com/od/comingout/a/population.htm (15 June 2010).

Pascoe, D. J. *Dude, You're a Fag: Masculinity and Sexuality in High School.* Berkeley: University of California Press, 2003.

Patterson, Romaine, and Patrick Hinds. *The Whole World Was Watching: Living in the Light of Matthew Shepard.* Los Angeles: Alyson Books, 2005.

Rogers, Jack. *Jesus, the Bible, and Homosexuality.* Louisville, Ky.: Westminster John Knox Press, 2009.

Stevens, Tracy. *How To Be a Happy Lesbian: A Coming Out Guide.* Asheville, N.C.: Amazing Dreams, 2006..

INDEX

ABOUT THE AUTHOR AND THE CONSULTANT

Bill Palmer has been involved in LGBT issues since he was Coordinator of his university's gay student alliance in the late 1970s and worked for many years for one of the largest academic publishers of LGBT books and journals in the world. Bill lives with his partner of thirty-plus years in upstate New York.

James T. Sears specializes in research in lesbian, gay, bisexual, and transgender issues in education, curriculum studies, and queer history. His scholarship has appeared in a variety of peer-reviewed journals and he is the author or editor of twenty books and is the Editor of the *Journal of LGBT Youth*. Dr. Sears has taught curriculum, research, and LGBT-themed courses in the departments of education, sociology, women's studies, and the honors college at several universities, including: Trinity University, Indiana University, Harvard University, Penn State University, the College of Charleston, and the University of South Carolina. He has also been a Research Fellow at Center for Feminist Studies at the University of Southern California, a Fulbright Senior Research Southeast Asia Scholar on sexuality and culture, a Research Fellow at the University of Queensland, a consultant for the J. Paul Getty Center for Education and the Arts, and a Visiting Research Lecturer in Brazil. He lectures throughout the world.